W9-AQC-124

✱ *For Emma* ✱
♥

Atheneum Books for Young Readers
An imprint of Simon & Schuster
Children's Publishing Division
1230 Avenue of the Americas
New York, New York 10020

Text copyright © 1996 by Edward Lear
Illustrations copyright © 1996 by Ian Beck
All rights reserved including the right of reproduction in
whole or in part in any form.

The text of this book is set in Goudy.

First Edition
Printed in Belgium
10 9 8 7 6 5 4 3 2 1

Library of Congress Catalog Card Number: 95-83849
ISBN 0-689-81032-6

Originally published in 1994 in Great Britain by
Transworld Publishers Ltd.

The
OWL
and the
PUSSY-CAT

EDWARD LEAR

Illustrated by
IAN BECK

Atheneum Books for Young Readers

MOOSEHEART
ELEMENTARY
SCHOOL LIBRARY
60539

The Owl and the Pussy-cat went to sea

In a beautiful pea-green boat,

They took some honey,

and plenty of money,

Wrapped up in a five-pound note.

The Owl looked up to the stars above,
And sang to a small guitar,

"O lovely Pussy! O Pussy my love,
What a beautiful Pussy you are,
You are,
You are!
What a beautiful Pussy you are!"

Pussy said to the Owl, "You elegant fowl!
How charmingly sweet you sing!

O let us be married! Too long we have tarried:
But what shall we do for a ring?"

They sailed away, for a year and a day

To the land where the Bong-tree grows

And there in a wood a Piggy-wig stood

With a ring at the end of his nose,
                    His nose,
                    His nose,
With a ring at the end of his nose.

"Dear Pig, are you willing to sell for one shilling

Your ring?" Said the Piggy, "I will."

So they took it away, and were married next day

By the Turkey who lives on the hill.

They dined on mince,

and slices of quince,

Which they ate with a runcible spoon;

And hand in hand, on the edge of the sand,

MOOSEHEART
ELEMENTARY
SCHOOL LIBRARY
60539

They danced by the light of the moon,